MARVEL
SPIDER-MAN
5 Minute Treasury

PaRragon

Bath · New York · Cologne · Melbourne · Delhi
Hong Kong · Shenzhen · Singapore

"The Story of Spider-Man" adapted by Alison Lowenstein.
Illustrated by Todd Nauck and Hi-Fi Design.
Based on the Marvel comic book series *Spider-Man*.

"The Sleepless Spider" written by Scott Peterson.
Illustrated by Rick Burchett and Hi-Fi Design.
Based on the Marvel comic book series *Spider-Man*.

"It's Electric" written by Alison Lowenstein.
Illustrated by Rick Burchett and Hi-Fi Design.
Based on the Marvel comic book series *Spider-Man*.

"The Claws of the Black Cat" written by Brendon Halpin.
Illustrated by Todd Nauck and Hi-Fi Design.
Based on the Marvel comic book series *Spider-Man*.

"Spider-Man at the Beach" written by Alison Lowenstein.
Illustrated by Lee Garbett and Hi-Fi Design.
Based on the Marvel comic book series *Spider-Man*.

"A Lizard on the Loose" written by Alison Lowenstein.
Illustrated by Lee Garbett and Hi-Fi Design.
Based on the Marvel comic book series *Spider-Man*.

"No Room for Debate" adapted from the original
story written by Nancy Lambert.
Illustrated by Ron Lim and Matt Milla.
Based on the Marvel comic book series *Spider-Man*.

"The Spectacular Spider-Fan" written by Bryan Q. Miller.
Illustrated by Lee Garbett and Hi-Fi Design.
Based on the Marvel comic book series *Spider-Man*.

"Mysterio Attacks" written by Michael Siglain.
Illustrated by Rick Burchett and Hi-Fi Design.
Based on the Marvel comic book series *Spider-Man*.

"A Job for Nova" written by Elizabeth Schaefer.
Illustrated by Scott Jeralds and Hi-Fi Design.
Based on the Marvel comic book series *Spider-Man*.

"The Fastest Web in the West" adapted from the
original story written by Arie Kaplan.
Illustrated by Ron Lim and Andy Troy.
Based on the Marvel comic book series *Spider-Man*.

"Climate Calamity" adapted from the original
story written by Andy Schmidt.
Illustrated by Khoi Pham and Andy Troy.
Based on the Marvel comic book series *Spider-Man*.

This edition published by Parragon Books Ltd in 2016

Parragon Books Ltd
Chartist House
15–17 Trim Street
Bath BA1 1HA, UK
www.parragon.com

ISBN 978-1-4748-4503-8

Printed in China

Contents

The Story of Spider-Man

Peter Parker was an average teenager who went to Midtown High School in New York City. He lived in Queens with his Aunt May and Uncle Ben. Until he was accidentally bitten by a radioactive spider, he was just like everybody else. In fact, he had it harder than most teenagers.

Peter was very hard-working and one of the smartest students in his school. But he wasn't very athletic and was often bullied.

One bully always seemed to go out of his way to pick on Peter. This bully was called Flash Thompson.

"Hey, you dropped your books," Peter heard Flash say to him as he walked down the hall.

"No, I didn't," Peter replied. Flash pushed him to the ground and Peter's books and papers fell around him.

School might have been tough for Peter, but he was happy at home. He was loved by his Aunt May and Uncle Ben. Peter's Uncle Ben always knew that Peter was going to do something special with his life.

"You are so smart, Peter, you can do anything," Uncle Ben told his nephew.

"Thanks Uncle Ben. I just want to be a scientist," Peter said humbly.

"A scientist is a very important job. Peter, science is power. And you should always remember – with great power comes great responsibility."

"You say that all the time Uncle Ben. How can I forget?"

Then one day Peter's life changed, on a school trip to the Science Hall. Peter was excited to see the scientists at work.

He was so distracted by the exhibits that he didn't even notice a spider pass through some radioactive waves and head straight towards him.

The radioactive spider bit Peter. He hadn't a clue what an amazing impact this would have on his life. Peter Parker would never be the same again.

After the bite, Peter discovered that he had spiderlike super powers. He could cling to walls, he was very strong, and he also had a 'spider-sense'. This meant that Peter was able to sense when trouble was near. These skills made Peter very powerful.

Peter wanted to keep his new powers a secret. He made himself a costume so that nobody would recognize him when he used his powers in public.

Peter worked hard to figure out how to use these new skills. Using his chemistry set, he made webs and tried shooting them in his bedroom.

"This is harder than I thought," Peter said to himself. "But once I get the hang of it, I will be able to do great things."

One day, Peter saw a poster advertising a wrestling theatre. Peter thought that taking part in a wrestling match would be the perfect way to test his powers. Peter used his costume as a disguise and won his first match easily. He soon began to wrestle for money. One night after a fight, the wrestling theatre was burgled. Since Peter and the owner didn't get along, Peter didn't help the owner catch the criminal.

Later that night, when Peter got home, he found out that a robber had burgled his home and killed Uncle Ben. Aunt May was devastated, and so was Peter.

The police officers told Peter not to worry. They had cornered the criminal at an old warehouse. Peter excused himself and went upstairs.

Peter suited up in his Spider-Man costume and swooped over the city. He was determined to avenge his uncle.

At last, Peter arrived at the warehouse. The thief was stunned. Then Spider-Man sprang into action.

As Spider-Man shot a web and trapped the crook, he got a good look at him – and realized that it was the same criminal he had let escape from the wrestling match!

If only he had stopped him then! If only he had not acted so selfishly! Peter vowed to help others from that moment on. He would never let anything like this happen again.

Just a month ago, Peter would have been busy studying in his bedroom at Aunt May and Uncle Ben's house, but not now. Peter remembered the words that his Uncle Ben always used to say: "With great power comes great responsibility."

The next day, the children at school started to talk about Spider-Man, and Peter listened to them in the halls.

"I think he's awesome," Flash said as he read a newspaper article about Spider-Man.

If only Flash knew that Peter was Spider-Man!

DAILY BUGLE

SPIDER-MAN
HERO OR MENACE?

That night, Spider-Man heard about a criminal on the loose in Manhattan. He swung across a bridge and into the streets to fight the villain, who was trying to rob a shop.

Spider-Man felt confident, because he had worked very hard at perfecting his abilities. He caught the criminal.

Spidey was now getting lots of attention. But for Peter, it wasn't about money or fame or any rewards his power could give him. Peter wanted to help others.

Peter Parker might seem like your normal teenager, but there is a part of him that makes him extremely special. He is a Super Hero and can scale buildings and spin webs. He is the Amazing Spider-Man!

The Sleepless Spider

Spider-Man has been called a great many things – amazing; spectacular; sensational. But today, no matter how hard Peter Parker tried, he was none of those. Today … Spider-Man was very, *very* sleepy.

For the last week, Peter couldn't sleep through the night. His dreams were troubling and sometimes downright spooky. And a week of nightmares makes for one sleepy crime-fighter.

Peter didn't think much of it, however, until one very long spider-yawn almost allowed Super Villain Shocker to ruin the Policeman's Ball, which was held every year to raise money for charity.

Spider-Man groggily swung into action just in time. He tied Shocker's hands together with webs before knocking the villain to the floor with a well-timed kick.

Spidey knew he needed to see a specialist,
someone who was truly an expert on dreams and the
human mind. And he knew just the doctor to call....

"Doctor Strange," Peter began, "I'm sorry
to interrupt, but I've been having trouble …"

"… SLEEPING!" Doctor Strange said as Spider-Man entered. Stephen Strange knew why Peter had visited him on that dark and stormy night. Strange had known about Peter's troubles long before Spider-Man had come to his doorstep. Doctor Strange threw his arms wide as he conjured the magical Eye of Agamotto.

"The Eye of Agamotto shows me that you've been having nightmares," Strange told Peter, "and now it will show me those nightmares."

Soon, Doctor Strange was able to see Spider-Man's dreams. In some, Spider-Man was back in primary school and had forgotten to wear his trousers! In others, he had nightmares about the Sinister Six villains winning every battle.

Doctor Strange could not only see the future and the past – he was able to see right into a man's very soul. And tonight, he intended to explore Peter's mind!

Strange told Peter, "Your sleep is interrupted not by the natural but by the supernatural. Your dreams are being invaded by the most dastardly of night-time threats – the villainous Nightmare himself!"

With a snap of his fingers, Strange placed Peter into a deep trance. With the help of the Eye, Strange took a deep breath, then dived into Peter's dreams.

Peter once again found himself trouserless in front of his entire class. And although he was embarrassed, he was no longer alone. Doctor Strange stood tall beside him, urging him to see the nightmare for what it truly was.

"The dream is yours to control," Strange told Peter.

Peter concentrated, and the class vanished. They were replaced by the master of bad dreams, Nightmare, and his trusty steed, Dreamstalker!

"The Sorcerer Supreme commands you to release your hold on this hero!" Strange shouted. But Nightmare simply laughed.

"I take power from dreams, Strange," Nightmare began, "and with a hero as strong as Spider-Man, I'll finally be great enough to defeat you!"

As Strange and Nightmare launched into magical combat
with each other, Peter knew he had to help the Sorcerer Supreme.
In a trance or not, Spider-Man had to lend a hand!

And he realized he knew just how to do it – by using the power
of his mind.

Peter thought and thought, as hard as he could. To his amazement, the dream around him began to change.

They weren't in Peter's school anymore, but on a giant chessboard, and Spider-Man was in control of the pieces.

"It would seem that Spider-Man is using the powers of his own dreams against you!" Strange declared to Nightmare.

Spidey played move after move, defeating Nightmare's pieces, until the villain was the only one left in play. Outnumbered, the villain retreated, leaving Peter's mind.

"You've won today, Strange, but you haven't seen the last of me!" Nightmare shouted as he rode Dreamstalker out of Peter's mind and back to his home in the shadow realm.

"I look forward to defeating you again." Strange smiled.

Peter woke with a start, pleased to find the
good Doctor waiting with a warm cup of tea.

Spidey swung home, changed into his pyjamas, and slipped under the sheets. There were no monsters under the bed, and the only things in his closet were his regular clothes and his spider-suits.

So, for the first time in what felt like weeks,
Peter Parker finally got a good night's sleep.

MARVEL
SPIDER-MAN

It's Electric

It was movie night at Aunt May's house. Peter had invited his friend Mary Jane, also known as MJ. As they all watched a film and shared some popcorn, the lights started to flicker and the TV switched off.

"Do you think it's the fuse box?" Aunt May asked.

Peter's spider-sense was telling him that it wasn't the fuse box. So he told them he'd check and headed to the basement, but he was really suiting up and getting ready to find the culprit behind this blackout.

Meanwhile, Jessica Drew was visiting New York City with her friend Lindsay.

As they walked across the Brooklyn Bridge, they took pictures of the skyline at dusk.

"Hey, it looks like the lights are out in the city," Lindsay said as Jessica took pictures.

Jessica, who was secretly Spider-Woman, had a feeling that trouble was brewing. When she saw Spider-Man swing through Manhattan, she knew she had to help. People on the bridge were pointing at Spider-Man, and Jessica was able to quietly suit up and join Spidey without her friend Lindsay noticing.

"Keep the lights on," Spider-Man demanded as he spotted Electro trying to destroy a telegraph pole.

"What, are you afraid of the dark?" Electro taunted as he unleashed a bolt of electricity at the Wall-Crawler.

Electro wanted to rob the gold vault at the Federal Reserve Bank. He was annoyed that Spider-Man was trying to stop him.

"Need some help?" Spider-Woman asked Spider-Man, as she used her super-human power to throw a large post van at Electro.

Spider-Man smiled. "Nice to see you're in town."

"This was supposed to be a holiday," she joked.

"A Spider-Man and a Spider-Woman. What a treat. I get to fry you both," Electro yelled.

"Doubtful, Electro. You're the one who is going to end up fried," Spidey told him.

Electro tried to escape from this powerful duo, and fired a massive bolt of electricity at a street lamp, causing it to blow. The explosion knocked Spider-Man back!

Spider-Woman confronted Electro, but the Super Villain unleashed another powerful blast. Spider-Woman tried to block it, but was shocked, and Electro escaped.

Electro managed to blast open the door to the
reserve and headed straight for the gold vault. But
Spider-Man and Spider-Woman were hot on his trail.

Electro fired a massive electric burst, temporarily blinding the heroes, and he ran to the vault where the gold was kept.

Electro turned the large gold wheel, opening the door to the vault.

"Game over, Electro." Spidey shot a web at Electro, attaching him to the wheel.

But Electro freed himself and

blasted the door open, saying,

"It's not over until I have my gold."

Spider-Woman knocked Electro on to the gold bricks, and Spider-Man webbed him down fast. "Now that the power is back up, every alarm in the city is going off. The police will be here in minutes," Spider-Woman told him.

"Thanks for teaming up with me, Spider-Woman," Spidey said.

"I'm so glad I was able to help. Now, I'm off to see the sights!" Spider-Woman replied as she hurried off to meet her friend.

"You missed some light show," Lindsay said to Jessica as she pointed towards Manhattan. "You could have taken some nice photos."

"I'm just glad to get some photos of the New York City skyline at night. It's so beautiful," Jessica said as she snapped some pictures.

Lindsay looked at the map. "Maybe tomorrow we should check out the Federal Reserve. I hear they offer a free tour."

"I've been there before, so let's go somewhere else," Jessica said with a smile.

"Sorry it took so long," Peter said as the lights came back on at Aunt May's house.

"You did a great job fixing the fuse box, Peter," Aunt May said with a smile.

"You're my Super Hero," Mary Jane said.

The Claws of the Black Cat

Late one night, two criminals, Boris and Bruno, were about to rob a bank. As Boris planted explosives, Bruno stood guard. They were surprised when a dark figure raced through the alleyway and landed beside them.

"Oh, no!" Bruno called out. "We have to run. It's Spider-Man!"

But the figure in the alley wasn't Spider-Man. It was the
Black Cat, a master thief.

"The police are on their way," the Black Cat said. "Do you
want to stay here and go to jail, or do you want to work for me?"

It wasn't a hard decision. They went with the Black Cat.

The next morning Peter Parker was at the *Daily Bugle*, the newspaper where he had a part-time job as a photographer. His boss, J. Jonah Jameson, also known as JJ, was very upset.

"Parker!" JJ yelled, "Spider-Man helped two bank robbers escape from the police last night. I want pictures!"

"Spider-Man wouldn't do something like that. I think there must be a mistake," Peter replied. He knew Spider-Man was innocent because Peter was Spider-Man, and he had been at home last night.

"I don't pay you to think. I pay you to take pictures," JJ barked.

Peter suited up as Spider-Man and searched for the real criminal who
had helped the bank robbers escape. As he perched on an American
flag that was sticking out from a rooftop, he saw a masked woman
dressed in black swing into police headquarters. He followed her.

He knew it! It was the Black Cat. Spider-Man had to act fast!

Spider-Man shot webs at the Black Cat, but she dodged them. The Black Cat hid in the shadows, safe from Spider-Man's webs.

Like a cat, she seemed to have nine lives and always ended up on her feet. She was also very fast.

Spidey lost her. He didn't notice her making a sneaky escape through a broken window.

Back at her hideout, the Black Cat told Bruno and Boris about her new plan.

"Boys, we have to break into jail."

"Break *into* jail?" Bruno was shocked. "That's crazy!"

"There's nothing to worry about – we won't be staying very long. I just need to free an old friend of mine. His name is Gadget, and he can build us all the tools we need to rob every bank in the city! The plans for the jail are in this box. Study them, so we can be prepared!" the Black Cat told the criminals.

They weren't pleased. Hearing the word *jail* made them shudder. They certainly didn't want to be a part of this plan, but there was no way out.

Peter Parker had set up a camera when he was chasing the Black Cat. He walked into the *Daily Bugle* with the pictures he had taken. Peter showed them to Jameson.

Peter said, "Spider-Man's chasing the Black Cat. She must have been the one who rescued those bank robbers from the police."

"They probably work together!" Jameson told Peter. "This is just two criminals trying to figure out how to split the loot."

A television in the newsroom of the *Daily Bugle* gave
Peter the answers he was looking for. "We repeat – there's
been a break-in at police headquarters," the newscaster said.
"Nothing was stolen except the plans for East River Prison."

Spidey swung into action, and he arrived at the prison just as the
Black Cat was lowering herself down the wall of the building on a rope.

"Here, kitty, kitty!" Spidey called.

The Black Cat spun around. "Back for more?" she asked. "You're in
trouble, young man. Now, Boris!"

Just then, Boris triggered the explosives he had put in place.
The wall of the prison fell apart, and Spidey fell right along with it.

Several officers pulled the rubble off Spider-Man. They
thanked him for trying to prevent the jailbreak, but Spider-Man
was embarrassed. The Black Cat had got away with Gadget.
However, Spidey already had a plan.

Spidey spoke to the guards and learned Gadget's real address. Then he went to Gadget's house. Gadget was really a retired engineer named Miles Stitchson.

When Spider-Man arrived, he found Boris and Bruno, and fired his web-shooters.

"Hey, why don't you guys hang around until the police get here?" Spidey said as he wrapped them up in webbing.

Just then the Black Cat opened the door. She was shocked to find Spider-Man waving back at her.

"It's time for you to give up," Spidey said to the Black Cat.

"Never!" the Black Cat cried. She leaped right at Spider-Man, but he ducked out of the way and she went flying over him. With incredible speed, she swung from the doorway, and landed on the roof of the house.

"Stick around!" Spidey said as the Black Cat stuck to the roof of the house. He had covered it in sticky webbing.

When the police arrived, they were very happy to arrest
Boris and Bruno. But the Black Cat had got away again!
She'd left her boots stuck to the roof and escaped.

"That cat really does have nine lives," Spider-Man said.
"I have a feeling we'll meet again."

"Thanks for capturing Bruno and Boris and leading us
back to Gadget," one of the policemen said to Spider-Man.

The next morning, Peter Parker walked into the offices of the *Daily Bugle*. "Well," he said to J. Jonah Jameson, "it looks like Spider-Man is a hero after all. He captured the bank robbers and the escaped prisoner."

"But he let the Black Cat get away! That Wall-Crawler may have everyone else fooled, but not me!" JJ yelled. "And who wrote this headline, anyway?"

Peter picked up a copy of the *Daily Bugle* and smiled. It read 'SPIDER-MAN: HERO!'

Spider-Man at the Beach

Mary Jane let out a scream as she rode the Cyclone roller coaster at the Coney Island amusement park.

"Have you ever been on anything so terrifying?" MJ asked as they exited the ride and walked towards the ice cream shop.

"Nope, that was scary all right. It really goes fast for an old roller coaster," Peter replied with a smile. If only MJ knew Peter was Spider-Man, and the night before he had climbed up a skyscraper and caught a villain. Then she'd know that he really wasn't scared on the ride!

Peter and MJ licked their ice cream cones and headed to the beach. As they made their way towards the water, Peter's spider-sense started to tingle. Beachgoers ran past them screaming.

Peter looked out and saw someone in the sand. It was Sandman, and he wasn't making a sandcastle – he was making trouble.

"I need to throw away this ice cream cone," Peter told MJ and sneaked off, quickly returning as Spider-Man. The people nearby stopped in awe as Spidey raced towards the villain.

"You might be made of sand, but this isn't your place in the sun," Spider-Man said as he shot a web at Sandman.

"A web isn't strong enough to hold me," Sandman said as he swung a fist at Spidey.

Spider-Man pushed Sandman. As Sandman fell back, Spidey was confident this would be an easy fight, until he heard a familiar laugh behind him.

Doctor Octopus grabbed at Spider-Man with one of his tentacles.

"I thought I smelled something fishy," Spider-Man said, pushing Dr Ock's tentacles away.

"It's over, Spider-Man. The city is mine." Dr Ock tried to grab Spider-Man again but Spidey jumped to dodge the tentacles.

Sandman got up, throwing a punch at Spider-Man, but Spidey avoided it. Battling two villains wasn't easy. The sun was strong and beating down on the beach, and Spider-Man was hot and thirsty. He wished he still had his ice cream cone as he fought tentacles and a menace made of sand.

Just then, Dr Ock's tentacles grabbed hold of Spidey and he couldn't break loose. Spider-Man was in trouble! Dr Ock smiled. "Now you are captured. There's no web you can spin that will get you out of this, Spider-Man."

Then Sandman got in on the action. Sandman punched Spider-Man with all of his might, knocking Spidey out of the tentacles and on to the sand.

"Look what you did!" Dr Ock yelled at Sandman. "You set him free."

"You two make a great team," Spider-Man joked as he leaped up.

Sandman ran towards the amusement park. Spidey knew he was up to no good. He wanted to chase Sandman, but he was still trying to stop Dr Ock. Battling two criminals was tricky, but he had to do it.

Spider-Man turned to Dr Ock. "Give up, Doc. It looks like your sandy partner in crime is now dust in the wind. He's *desert*-ed you."

"Deserted. Very funny. You were always one with a pun."

"I aim to please." Spidey smiled as he fired a web at Dr Ock's face.

"I never needed Sandman. I have my own plan, which he never knew about. I'm going to create a huge wave that will flood the city! Then I will take charge!" Dr Ock yelled.

The waves were getting higher and higher, and Spider-Man was worried they would start to flood the beach. He shot as many webs as he could in an attempt to stop Dr Ock.

Spider-Man shot four more webs and wound them round all of Dr Ock's tentacles as the villain fell to the ground with a thud, trapped and helpless.

"Gotcha. You're not going to slip out of this grip," Spidey said. Dr Ock couldn't move.

"This isn't going to work," Dr Ock said, trying to use his tentacles to break free.

"Looks like it has. You're stuck in the sun. Bet you wish you had packed some sunscreen," Spidey joked.

Meanwhile, Sandman was grabbing all of the cash from the ticket booths at the amusement park. Sandman grew more excited as the bag of loot got heavier. He was going to be rich, and Spider-Man was too distracted with Dr Ock to fight him. His plan was working.

As Sandman grabbed money from the last booth, Spider-Man jumped down from the Ferris wheel and leaped at him.

"Buying a ticket to the fun house?" Spidey asked as he knocked Sandman down. Sandman's bag of cash fell open and the money started to blow away in the wind.

"Looks like you're blowing your money," Spider-Man said as he shot a web at Sandman.

Cornered, Sandman looked round for Dr Ock.

"If you're looking for the doctor, he is caught up in a web," said Spidey. Then the Web-Slinger fired even more webs at Sandman. "Seems like you might have had different plans, but you both ended up in the same place."

Spidey attached a webbed Sandman to the Ferris wheel.
"It's your lucky day, Sandy. You get a free ride. Too bad your
friend is stuck on the beach," Spidey said. Then he remembered
MJ. He had to find her in the crowd.

As the crowd made their way back to the beach, they cheered for Spider-Man. As he swung over all the people, Spidey wasn't thinking about all of the attention – he was too concerned with finding MJ.

After searching the crowd, he saw her in front of the ice cream shop.

"Peter, where were you?" MJ asked.

"I went to throw away my cone, and then I saw all the commotion and came looking for you."

"I was in the ice cream shop," MJ replied. "Thankfully, you're safe. Were you able to see Spider-Man?"

"I just saw him for a second. I wanted to stay out of trouble." Peter smirked.

"Want to go on some rides?" MJ asked.

"Sure – just not the Ferris wheel," Peter said with a grin.

A Lizard on the Loose

Peter Parker anxiously read an article about the Lizard that was splashed across the cover of that day's *Daily Bugle*. Peter knew that it meant his friend Dr Curtis Connors was in trouble.

Peter also knew that his boss, J. Jonah Jameson, would be angry that he didn't have exclusive snapshots of the Lizard. JJ relied on Peter for these types of photos.

When Peter walked into the *Daily Bugle*, J. Jonah Jameson called him into his office.

"Parker, the Lizard is on the loose and I need pictures," JJ demanded. "I don't care if you have to camp out in a swamp. I want a shot for the front page. And I also want a picture of Spider-Man fighting the Lizard," JJ said with a grin. JJ knew he was asking for the impossible, but he expected perfection.

"I'm your man. I'll get those shots," Peter told his boss.

Earlier, Dr Connors' wife was very upset. She had seen her husband mixing up a strange formula that week. She knew that he was trying to create a serum that would help him grow back his missing arm, but she also knew that it came with a serious side effect. It turned Dr Connors into an evil villain called the Lizard.

Spider-Man found Mrs Connors sitting on her porch.

She was staring at a picture of her husband.

"I wish he didn't care about growing that arm back."

She looked at Spidey with concern.

"I'll find him," Spidey told Mrs Connors. "Don't worry."

"You need to bring him to the lab and feed him the antidote."

"Got it! He won't be a lawless lizard for much longer. Soon he will be back to being good old Dr Connors."

Spidey searched all through New York City and finally spotted the Lizard.
Spider-Man chased him into an ice cream shop, hoping to lock the cold-blooded
beast in a freezer, which would take away the Lizard's strength. But the Lizard
escaped, crashing through the window.

"I'm not a fan of frozen treats," the Lizard called out to Spidey.

"If you try to run from me, you're going to be on a Rocky Road," Spidey taunted.

The Lizard stomped through the streets, creating a wave of destruction,
crushing car windows and damaging shopfronts.

Spidey trailed behind the Lizard as they made their way up the building where Dr Connors had his lab.

"Once you go in, you're not coming out," Spidey said as he scaled the side of the building.

The Lizard tried to knock Spidey down with his powerful tail, but it didn't work. The Lizard's roar echoed through the streets of the city.

People crowded around to see the excitement. Spidey was going to save the day!

Spider-Man made his way into the lab, grabbing the antidote. The Lizard crashed through the door, followed by a group of angry reptiles. Spidey knew that the Lizard must have given them something to make them so vicious. Suddenly, a snake slithered through the door, making its way towards Spidey.

"Yikes," Spider-Man called out as a small lizard bit his foot and a snake coiled itself round his leg.

Spidey quickly fired webs at the Lizard as more reptiles attacked.

The Lizard fought off the webs, pushing Spider-Man back and swinging his tail at Spidey.

The team of reptiles attacked again, and Spider-Man didn't know if he was going to be able to fight both the Lizard and the many cold-blooded fiends that surrounded him.

Spider-Man was fighting for his life when the Lizard threw a filing cabinet at him. Spidey fell down in pain. His body ached and he didn't know if he would be able to get up.

"Ouch!" Spidey called out, "Dr Connors, do you realize what you are doing? You have to stop the Lizard!"

But it was pointless. Dr Connors had no control once the Lizard was unleashed. You couldn't reason with him – you just needed to give him the antidote.

Spidey eyed the antidote as the Lizard seized the opportunity to attack him. He ordered the reptiles to hold Spidey down as the Lizard threw a bunch of powerful blows.

Spider-Man tried hard to fight back, but was careful that they didn't bump into the antidote. He didn't want to spill it. Finally Spidey broke free, grabbed the antidote, and poured it on to the Lizard's rough tongue.

Within seconds, the Lizard began to fade and Dr Connors reappeared. Spider-Man was very happy to see his friendly and familiar face. The beasts had been tamed, and Mrs Connors would be happy to have her husband back home.

"Wow, what happened?" Dr Connors asked.

"It's a long story." Spidey sighed.

Soon, Mrs Connors had her husband back
and J. Jonah Jameson had his front-page spread.
Everyone was happy!

Peter came home to one of Aunt May's amazing home-cooked meals. "How was your day, Peter?" Aunt May asked.

Peter didn't even know where to begin. Aunt May didn't know that Peter was Spider-Man, and he certainly couldn't tell her about his fight with the Lizard. "Don't forget to save room for dessert, Peter," Aunt May said as Peter finished his soup. "I bought some ice cream. Your favourite, Rocky Road."

No Room for Debate

Peter Parker tried to calm his nerves as he entered Oscorp Tower's fancy new media centre. Oscorp was hosting the big debate match between Midtown High and Coles Academic, and Peter was in the first group to compete.

Peter got settled at the Midtown High table.

"For our first match," the announcer said, "Peter Parker, representing Midtown High, and Kamala Khan, representing Coles Academic."

Peter nervously looked over at his opponent.

Just as the announcer opened her mouth to share the topic of the debate, the lights went dark. The audience murmured and there were shouts of confusion before a raspy voice boomed over the intercom:

"I'd like to announce a surprise guest ... me!"

It was Green Goblin!

Peter knew it was time for Spidey to make an appearance.
He fumbled in the shadows, looking for a safe spot to change.

"I need Spider-Man for a few tests," the Goblin growled.
"So here's something to debate: do you think capturing an entire
audience will lure Spider-Man into my trap?"

The audience screamed. Spider-Man prepared to swing out
and surprise the Goblin, but someone grabbed his arm in the dark.

"Stay down – let me handle him," a girl whispered.

"I can stop him," Peter replied. "I'm Spider –"

Just then there was a loud cracking sound. An eerie green force field began to surround the horrified audience.

There was a deep humming as the force field got brighter and brighter, and then with a *SNAP* the audience was gone – and so was Green Goblin!

The lights flickered back on.

"Spider-Man!" the girl said.

Spidey looked at her and gasped. "Ms Marvel?"

"I could have saved the audience if I hadn't been trying to stop you," she sighed. "I'd love to chat, but I've got a Goblin to catch."

"Wait a second," Spidey said. "Goblin set the trap for me, so obviously I should be the one to handle it."

"Maybe we should work together," Ms Marvel suggested.

The lights flickered again. But when Spider-Man and Ms Marvel looked more closely, they realized the whole room was flickering a little.

There was a bright flash. Suddenly, they saw the debate room as it really was – a windowless steel cell! There was one door, but it had no handle and was shut tight.

"The Goblin must have built this trap under Oscorp's new media centre and used holograms to disguise it as the debate room," Ms Marvel said.

Using her shape-shifting super powers, Ms Marvel slid through the crack under the door.

In a few moments, the door opened with a hiss. Ms Marvel was waiting on the other side; she was back to her normal shape.

"Ready to grab a Goblin?" she asked.

Spidey passed through the door to join Ms Marvel.

Ms Marvel held a finger to her lips. "Listen...."

They heard shouts for help.

"I have an idea," Ms Marvel said.

Ms Marvel smiled and started typing into the hologram control panel on the wall – the same one that had created the holographic debate room. "You get the Goblin's attention."

Spider-Man shouted down the hall, "Hey, you green monster, your favourite Wall-Crawler is here!"

With a *WHOOSH*, the Green Goblin sped down the corridor on his glider. He stopped short at the cell doorway. Spider-Man and Ms Marvel were waiting for him inside.

"A two-for-one deal – what a surprise!" the Green Goblin said with a sneer.

The Green Goblin lobbed some pumpkin bombs towards the
Super Heroes. The bombs exploded at their feet, but to his surprise,
Spidey and Ms Marvel were unharmed. The Goblin's rage grew. He
fired a dozen more pumpkin bombs at the duo. Still nothing.

But Spidey and Ms Marvel did *flicker* ever so slightly....

"Huh?" the Goblin swung around to face the door, where the real Spider-Man and Ms Marvel were waiting. They'd used holograms of themselves to trick him while they hid round the corner! The duo quickly shoved Green Goblin deep into the cell.

"How does it feel to be caught in your own trap, Goblin?" Spidey asked.

After everyone had been freed, Peter rejoined the other students, who were buzzing over the day's events.

Kamala smiled. "So, seeing Spider-Man was pretty cool...."

"Yeah, but not as cool as seeing Ms Marvel," he replied.

"Okay, I won't argue with that," she said, laughing.

They shook hands and said goodbye, unaware of each other's secret identities.

The Spectacular Spider-Fan

It was October 31ˢᵗ, and, as he did every Halloween, Peter Parker was helping Aunt May hand out sweets to the trick-or-treaters. As group after group of ghosts and witches, astronauts and Super Heroes came and went, Aunt May couldn't help but remember simpler times.

"Peter, I remember how excited you would get when you were little," she said. "You always loved running around in costumes."

I still do, Peter thought, hiding a secret smile.

But then, just as Aunt May dropped another heaped handful of sweets into the children's bags, Peter's spider-sense started tingling. Danger was near!

Meanwhile, just up the road, little David Dangle and his friends
were ringing doorbells and raking in the goods – chocolate, liquorice,
you name it, they had collected it.

David, as it happened, was dressed as his favourite hero – he had
been waiting all year to dress up as the Spectacular Spider-Man!

Unfortunately, little David Dangle's timing was terrible….

Other children started shouting in the distance. David and his friends spun round, alarmed. The villainous Hobgoblin was flying through the night, stealing bags of sweets, left, right and centre!

"You aren't *really* Spider-Man, are you?" Hobgoblin shrieked, whirling down towards David. "You're short, you're scrawny, and you're *certainly* no hero."

"I am tonight!" David replied. He knew he was no match for the villain, but had to do whatever he could to keep his neighbourhood safe.

"Run, you guys! I can handle this!" David shouted, standing his ground as Hobgoblin swooped closer.

Hobgoblin stopped dead in his tracks, hovering right in front of the tiny hero.

"Robbing banks makes me ever so hungry," the villain snarled.

Then, with one swift swipe, Hobgoblin ripped David's bag of sweets right from the boy's back!

"I won't let you get away with this!" David said as

he targeted the villain with his toy web-shooters.

David sprayed and sprayed. He covered

Hobgoblin's face with fake webs!

But Hobgoblin easily shrugged off the foam, a sneer curling his lips.

"You know, you're just as foolish as the *real* Spider-Man," Hobgoblin chuckled.

"I'll take that as a compliment!" a strong voice called out from above.

It was Spider-Man – the *real*, true,
Fantastic, Sensational, Amazing Spider-Man!
Spidey swung past, grabbing David and
carrying him to safety, far from the villain's reach.

"There's nothing foolish about being a brave, friendly neighbourhood Spider-Fan," Peter began, "but take it from a genuine Web-Head – this kind of trouble needs to be handled by grown-ups!"

"You've got it, Spidey!" David said. He knew the hero was right.

Peter made David promise to stay safe, then lunged back out into the night sky. Spidey shot a web line, diving straight for Hobgoblin.

"Don't think I haven't prepared for this," Hobgoblin
challenged. He reached into his bag and hurled a handful of
razor-sharp, bat-shaped ninja weapons right at the Wall-Crawler.
Spidey twirled around the blades with ease … but his web
line didn't. The bat-blades snapped his web, and sent the hero
hurtling towards the hard concrete below!

"Grab the clothesline, Spider-Man!" David shouted from above.

"Great idea, Spider-Fan!" Peter called back. Spidey took hold of the clothesline as he fell. Shirts, jumpers and dresses flew left and right as he swung down into the villain. Spider-Man knocked Hobgoblin from his glider with a mighty kick!

It wasn't long before the police arrived to deal with the defeated villain. Spider-Man made sure he returned all of the bags of sweets to their rightful owners.

"Happy Halloween everyone!" Spidey said as he swung off into the night.

Exhausted and exhilarated, David soon returned home from his night of adventure. He gave his mum with a giant bear hug. "How was your night?" she asked.

David couldn't hide his smile, grinning from ear to ear.

"Mum," he said, "my night was *amazing*!"

Next year, Peter thought, maybe I'll go trick-or-treating as my new hero.

And just who was that new hero?

It was a little Spider-Fan named David Dangle!

Mysterio Attacks

*T*HWIP! Spider-Man shot a web across Fifth Avenue and swung past the Empire State Building on his way towards the *Daily Bugle*. Peter Parker was late for work, and the only things that could get him there in time were his web-shooters.

"Great," Peter said to himself as he fired another web line. "If I'm late for work again, Mr Jameson is going to explode!"

Just then, an explosion of green and purple smoke erupted from the top floor of the *Daily Bugle* building!

"Yikes! I didn't think he'd *literally* explode!" Spidey said as he saw the blast. "I had better get in there to see if anyone needs help."

Landing on the side of the building, Spider-Man crawled up the wall, through a window and into the smoky office – but the office was empty!

That's when Spidey heard a booming voice coming from the newsroom and his spider-sense started to tingle.

"Now that I have your attention," the bizarre voice began, "you will all be witness to the total destruction of the *Daily Bugle!*"

Spider-Man recognized that voice – it was his enemy Mysterio, the master of illusion!

Spidey creeped to the door and opened it a crack so that he could see what was going on. The menacing Mysterio was holding J. Jonah Jameson by the collar and addressing the staff.

"No one can help you, Jameson, not even Spider-Man!" the villain hissed.

"That's my cue!" Spidey said as he lunged through the door and launched himself at the villain.

Spider-Man caught Mysterio by surprise and the two tumbled to the ground, locked in combat! As the Super Hero and Super Villain continued to fight, Jameson crawled to the exit but was surprised to see that all the doors had been locked from the outside.

They were trapped!

"The Amazing Spider-Man!" Mysterio began. "Right on time ... to meet your doom!"

Mysterio raised his arms and the newsroom filled with thick green smoke. Then the villain disappeared into the fog right before everyone's eyes!

"Meet *my* doom?" Spider-Man said. "What do you suppose he meant by *that*?"

Mysterio's voice suddenly echoed across the room. "When I first appeared, J. Jonah Jameson promised that he could give Spider-Man to me," the villain said. "Instead, I was defeated by Spider-Man … and now, you will *all* pay – starting with Jameson!"

Spidey knew he had to act fast! Just as Mysterio appeared from the smoke, Spider-Man fired a web line and swung towards the villain.

With unbelievable strength and speed, the Amazing Spider-Man kicked Mysterio in the chest and then fired another web line at Jameson, sticking him to the wall.

"Sorry to disappoint you, Mysterio, but I don't have plans to meet my doom for at least another 60 or 70 years!" Spidey said.

Spider-Man stood above the trapped Mysterio and removed the villain's domed helmet. But Spidey was shocked at the person he saw beneath the mask: it was Peter Parker!

"Parker!" Jameson yelled. "*You're* Mysterio?"

Mysterio was a master of disguise, but only Spider-Man knew that the villain wasn't *really* Peter Parker. *This must have been the disguise he was going to use in order to escape*, Spidey thought. But how was Spider-Man going to save everyone in the *Daily Bugle* and prove that Mysterio wasn't Peter?

While all these thoughts ran through Spidey's mind, the villain leaped forwards and attacked!

Ow! Spidey thought to himself as he picked himself up off the floor. As Mysterio delivered another blow, Spider-Man rolled across the smoky room.

Spidey looked round the office, and realized that everyone was at work – except for one person. The only person who wasn't there was the person who was late – Peter Parker. *That's why Mysterio used me for his disguise,* Spidey thought. And that gave the Wall-Crawler an idea!

Spidey jumped across the room and crawled along the wall, completely hidden by the smoke. He grabbed a hoodie off a desk, wrapped it round himself, and removed his mask.

Just then, the real Peter Parker appeared through the smoke. "Hey, guys. Sorry I'm late!"

Mysterio turned, shocked. "No! How did *you* get in?" the villain shouted.

"*Two* Parkers?" Jameson said, confused. "Next there will be two Spider-Men!"

"Not if *I* have anything to say about it!" Mysterio yelled.

The appearance of the real Peter Parker had worked. While everyone was distracted, Peter ducked beneath the smoke, put his mask back on, and charged at Mysterio.

Firing both web-shooters again and again, the Amazing Spider-Man captured Mysterio in a giant spiderweb for all to see.

Then with a *CRASH*, the police finally broke into the newsroom, just as Spider-Man jumped out of the nearest window. "Here you go, boys," Spidey said to the police as he swung away. "One gift-wrapped Super Villain, courtesy of you-know-who!"

A few minutes later, the real Peter Parker entered the newsroom. J. Jonah Jameson, who was still stuck to the side of the wall, looked down at his star photographer. "Parker," JJ said, "You're late!"

Peter sighed. It was just another day at the office for Peter Parker ... and your friendly neighbourhood Spider-Man!

A Job for Nova

Peter Parker didn't usually have time to hang around – but here he was, hanging from the top of a skyscraper with nothing to do. No Super Villains to fight, no citizens to save, no sirens to follow. It had been like this for a whole week.

The Amazing Spider-Man … bored.

I bet Iron Man never runs out of things to do, Spider-Man thought, staring at his reflection.

He started doodling on the side of the building to keep himself busy.

Suddenly, Spider-Man's spider-sense began to tingle. "Finally," Spidey said, "some action!" With a practised ease, Spider-Man leaped down towards the street and caught his reflection in a shop window.

"Maybe it's Sandman," Peter said, imagining himself fighting the villain. "I could do with a day at the beach."

Spider-Man followed the sirens all the way to City Hall. There, he found a team of police officers looking up at the building's roof.

"Spider-Man! Thank goodness you're here! Sandman has kidnapped the mayor!" Just then, Sandman appeared on the top of the building!

Yes! It is Sandman! Spidey thought.

"Don't worry! I'll be back with the mayor before you can say – " But before Spider-Man could say anything, a bolt of blue light flashed through the sky.

"It's a bird!"

"It's a plane!"

"No, it's Nova," Spider-Man said, disappointed.

"Nova?" the police officer asked Spider-Man.

"A Super Hero with crazy space powers. He can fly, lift super-heavy things and steal the spotlight in less than three seconds flat."

Spider-Man knew that being a Super Hero meant more than getting attention. It was a privilege – and a responsibility.

But there was something about Nova that drove Spider-Man crazy.

Spider-Man quickly realized that the police officer was much more interested in the exciting fight between Sandman and Nova.

"Get ready to taste my fist, Nova!" Sandman roared.

"I doubt it! Fighting you is like a day at the beach!" Nova replied.

"Man – he even stole my joke!" Spider-Man said under his breath.

With a supersonic punch, Nova knocked Sandman out. The policemen cheered.

"I don't know what we would have done without you, Nova," the mayor said.

Fortunately, Spidey didn't have to listen to Nova's fans for long. His spidey-sense
began to tingle again. Someone needed help!

Spider-Man swung his way across town to a large bank.

Three men in masks were stealing money from the safe.

Spider-Man swung in to stop them.

"Oh, no, it's the Spider!" one of the robbers said.

"Actually, it's Spider-*Man*," Peter said, as he used his web-shooter to knock the stolen money out of the robber's hands.

Spider-Man led the three robbers outside. But just then, Nova flew down, carrying a car in one hand and a very worried fourth robber in the other.

Peter had forgotten about the getaway car!

"Looks like you lost something, Spider," Nova said.

"Spider-MAN!" Peter said. But no one heard him. They were all cheering for Nova.

The next day, Peter was back to doing nothing. *At least I'm improving my artistic skills*, he thought, as he put the finishing touches on a Nova web sculpture.

He was so busy admiring his handiwork, that he almost didn't hear the sirens. Peter looked down and saw police cars racing uptown.

I'll just let Nova deal with that, Spider-Man thought.

But Spider-Man couldn't ignore his spider-sense, and more importantly, he couldn't ignore people in trouble. He quickly jumped off the roof and swung towards the sirens.

Nova was fighting the Lizard on Brooklyn Bridge. The Lizard looked tired, but Nova wasn't even breaking a sweat!

Well, I guess I'm not needed here after all, Spider-Man thought.

He turned round, about to head back home, when he felt a tug on his costume. He looked down and saw a little boy.

"Mr Spider-Man, sir. Can you help me?"

Spider-Man kneeled down. "Sure. What do you need?"

"I can't find Puddles anywhere – he's my dog."

Spider-Man sighed. Dog-catching wasn't exactly as epic as fighting the Lizard on a crowded bridge. But Spider-Man was happy that he could help somebody.

"All right, where did you last see him?" he asked.

Before long, Spider-Man found the boy's dog hiding in some bushes near the bridge. "Looks like he didn't like the noise of all that fighting," Spider-Man said, as he gave the dog back to the young boy.

"Thanks, Spider-Man!" the boy said.

The boy glanced back at the fight on the bridge. "Mr Spider-Man, do you think Nova will be okay?"

"Nova's going to be just fine. He's a hero."

"Just like you?"

"Yes, just like me."

The boy smiled. That smile made Spider-Man feel as good as a thankful mayor or a cheering crowd. Well, almost as good. Cheering crowds *were* pretty hard to beat.

As Spider-Man jumped into the air he felt his spider-sense tingling.

"Here we go again." He smiled to himself. Nova couldn't possibly beat him to the villain this time … right?

The Fastest Web in the West

Peter Parker was having an excellent day. He had just aced a history test on the Wild West. It was Peter's favourite topic, and he loved to imagine himself as a cowboy, fighting outlaws like Billy the Kid.

Peter had grown up watching classic western movies with his Uncle Ben, so he thought he was an expert on the Old West.

After school, Spider-Man zipped over to his friend Black Widow's tower. He had agreed to house-sit for her, while she went on a mission.

As Black Widow gave Spidey a list of chores, he found himself staring at an old pocket watch. Widow explained that the watch was actually a mysterious object she had found. "Don't touch it," she warned.

After Spidey had finished his chores, he was bored. He peered at the pocket watch. *It's just a watch. What could go wrong?* Spidey thought. The Wall-Crawler lifted the watch's lid. *POP!* He disappeared.

Spider-Man reappeared in a ramshackle town. Suddenly, he heard a commotion, and turned to see two horsemen chasing after three bandits ... heading straight towards him!

One of the crooks bumped into Spidey. A crowd gathered around. Pointing at the teenage robber, the onlookers yelled, "It's Billy the Kid!"

Spider-Man realized that he was in the Old West! The pocket watch must have been a time machine. But Spidey had lost it in the confusion!

As Billy ran away from the crowd, a scrap of paper fell out of his pocket. Spidey unfolded it. It was a map of stagecoach routes, with notes scribbled on it. Billy was going to rob the stagecoach at Romita Canyon!

Spider-Man decided to stop Billy. Just then, he felt a hand on his shoulder.

"Howdy there. I'm Sheriff Fury," the man said.

Spider-Man talked like a movie cowboy to impress Sheriff Fury. "I'm the biggest, baddest galoot west of the Pecos," he declared.

"I'm not sure what that nonsense means, but I don't like masked bandits," Sheriff Fury said. "You must have been helping Billy!"

Before Spidey could respond, Fury's sidekick, Deputy Coulson, slammed into him. Spider-Man decided not to fight back. He didn't want to be misunderstood further. Spidey soon found himself in jail. But he had to stop the stagecoach robbery!

Using his super strength, Spider-Man bent the jail cell bars apart and walked out. Sheriff Fury was speechless. To prove that he meant no harm, Peter walked back into his cell. This convinced the sheriff that Spidey was a good guy.

The Wall-Crawler explained that he was a hero from the future who had special powers. Spider-Man showed Billy's map to Sheriff Fury. Fury told Spidey to go and stop Billy while the lawman stayed to protect the town.

Soon Spider-Man reached Romita Canyon. Billy had the stagecoach's wealthy passengers kneeling on the ground. His henchmen, Charlie and Tom, were looting a chest of valuables taken from the stagecoach.

Spider-Man fired webbing at Billy's hands, sticking them together. Charlie and Tom tossed their lassos at Spidey, and the Wall-Crawler dodged the ropes. But Peter couldn't keep this up forever. The crooks were lasso experts. What would he do?

Then Spider-Man had an idea. Maybe he could make a lasso, too! Fashioning his web into a makeshift lasso, Spidey bounced from bandit to bandit. He tied up Tom, then Charlie, and finally Billy the Kid!

Spider-Man delivered the criminals to Sheriff Fury. As the
lawman took them, Billy yelped, "There's a snake in my boot!"

Billy yanked off his boot. Both the snake and the pocket watch
fell out! Billy had stolen the watch when he and Spider-Man had
bumped into each other outside the bank.

Spidey decided it was time to go back home.

Spider-Man arrived back in the 21ˢᵗ century with a loud *POP!*
He was overjoyed to be home. But he felt bad that he had
broken his promise to Black Widow. He wrote her a note.

The note read, "Sorry I didn't listen. I guess when you said not to touch the pocket watch, you meant it." Then Spider-Man placed something beside the note. It was a *Daily Bugle* newspaper he'd picked up just before he'd left the Old West. And Spidey was on the front page!

Climate Calamity

There was always something for Spider-Man to do before he could get back to being regular old Peter Parker! On one wintry day, the evil Scorpion kidnapped J. Jonah Jameson – because the villain liked JJ even less than Spidey did!

"You're to blame for the Scorpion's attack, Spider-Man!" JJ yelled. But Spider-Man saved the day, even though it meant helping someone he didn't like. That's what heroes do!

"Thanks, Spider-Man!" one of the police officers said.

JJ immediately shouted, "Yeah! Thanks for nothing, Web-Head!"

The snow was coming down harder than before. Spider-Man
needed to get home to Aunt May to make sure she was okay –
and of course, to eat a big bowl of her famous chicken soup.

On his way home, Spidey heard someone calling for help from a playground. "My work is never done," Spider-Man said.

"Spider-Man! Skyler is stuck in the pipe," a young boy told Spidey. "She went in through the top, but she didn't know that the ends were blocked by snow. She can't get out!"

Spidey dropped into the pipe and found Skyler, cold and scared. "Don't worry," Spidey said. "I'll get you out of here!"

Spider-Man pulled Skyler out of the pipe and returned her safely to the ground.

"Thanks, Spidey," Skyler said as Charlie, the eldest boy, gave her a big hug.

"It sure is getting cold. Let's get a move on," said Spider-Man.

Another boy called Gavin looked round, a little confused. "You mean ... you're going to help us get home?"

"I wouldn't be a friendly neighbourhood Spider-Man if I didn't," Spidey said. "Now bundle up! You're not the only ones who need rescuing today!"

On their way to Gavin's house, the children spotted Captain Stacy's police car caught in a snowdrift. "Well, we can't let the police get stuck in the snow when they're supposed to be helping everyone else," Spider-Man declared.

He spun his powerful webs and towed Captain Stacy's car free.

The children sat on top of the car and laughed with delight as it moved slowly through the snow!

After dropping Gavin off, the Wall-Crawler and the remaining six children started to cross the Queensboro Bridge. But the road was slippery, and the fire department needed help melting the ice.

Spider-Man had an idea! The children swung up and around on his webs, sprinkling salt across the road. Riley yelled, "Now that's how Team Spidey melts ice!"

As the group left Skyler and Riley's house, Oliver noticed an elderly man shivering by himself. "Is there anything we can do to help that man, Spidey?" Oliver asked. Spidey thought for a moment.

Then he spun a coat, some mittens and a hat out of webs!

"I hope these help keep you warm, sir," Spidey said. The man was happy to have the extra layers.

When Spider-Man saw a little dog shivering in an alley near Miles and Ellie's home, he stopped to help.

And the children helped, too! It turned out that helping others was a great way to keep their minds off the cold. As Spidey made an igloo for the dog out of his webs, Miles kept the puppy warm and Charlie got a blanket for it. Oliver found some food, and Ellie named the puppy Hazel. Ellie even made a sign for the puppy's new house that read HAZEL'S HOME SWEET HOME!

Spider-Man and the children were almost home. But there was just
time to have some fun in the snow. Charlie started a snowball fight,
and the children even made a friendly neighbourhood snowman!

Oliver and Charlie were the last of the children to get home, and their parents were so glad to see them!

"Mum! Dad! Spider-Man got Skyler out of a pipe! And then we helped firefighters! And police cars! Can you believe it?" Oliver said.

Charlie and Oliver waved goodbye to their hero. Spider-Man was so proud of the children. They were heroes, too!

After a quick change out of his costume, Peter Parker
finally arrived home to Aunt May. But Peter knew he was late,
late, late! Just as he started to say he was sorry, Aunt May said,
"Now, don't you go apologizing to me, Peter!"

"You should know by now that I can take care of myself," Aunt May said. "But it looks like you're catching a cold! Sit down and let me look after you."

Peter had spent the day as Spider-Man, playing hero to people all over the city. But even Super Heroes need to be rescued sometimes – and Aunt May would always be Spidey's hero.